THE
PURPLE HAT

Tracey Campbell Pearson

Farrar · Straus · Giroux

New York

E
PEA

Published simultaneously in Canada by HarperCollinsCanadaLtd
Color separations by Prestige Graphics
Printed and bound in the United States of America by Berryville Graphics
First edition, 1997

Library of Congress Cataloging-in-Publication Data
Pearson, Tracey Campbell.
The purple hat / Tracey Campbell Pearson. — 1st ed.
p.   cm.
[1. Hats—Fiction.]   I. Title.
PZ7.P323318Pu   1997   [E]—dc20   96-3116 CIP AC

For Catherine

The day the catalogue came in the mail, Annie grabbed it first.

"You can keep it," Ben said.

And she did.

Annie took it with her everywhere and showed it to everyone.
"Isn't it lovely?" she said, pointing to the picture of the girl in the
purple hat.

"It would go very nicely with my purple coat," she told her mom.

"Very," her mom said.

"Just right with my purple shoes," she told her dad.

"Just right," he said.

One day, a package arrived in the mail. It was addressed to Annie.

"What's in it?" asked Ben.

"I don't know," said Annie.

"Open it!" said Ben.

Inside the box was the purple hat. It was perfect.

Annie spent the rest of the day in her room, admiring herself in her new hat.

Ben spent the rest of the day in his room, reading.

The next morning, when Annie came to breakfast, she was completely purple.

"How lovely," said her dad.

"How purple," said her brother.

"Are you sure you want to wear your new hat to school?" asked her mom.

Annie walked to school very slowly so everyone could see her new purple hat.

Ben ran right by her.

When Annie got to her classroom, everyone admired her new purple hat. Then Mrs. Bows gathered the class for share.

"Today we have a special guest," she said and introduced them to Mrs. Erb.

Mrs. Erb said, "You can just call me the Bird Lady!"
First, she shared her bird calls.
Next, they all made binoculars.   After snack, everyone lined up . . .
"Shhhhhhh," whispered Mrs. Bows. "So you can hear the birds."

The class quietly followed the Bird Lady out the door, into the woods, and out again.

After school, Annie flew home like a bird.

By the time Ben arrived, she was up a tree, building a nest.

"Where is it?" he asked.

"Where's what?" she said.

"The hat!"

Annie screamed.

That evening, Annie's family tried everything they could to get her mind off the purple hat and to get her out of the tree.

She finally cried herself to sleep. Her dad carried her down
from the tree and tucked her into her own bed.

Annie dreamed about purple hats all night long.

She woke up exhausted.

Before school began, Annie and her family looked for the purple hat. Mrs. Bows helped, too.

At recess, Ben organized a search party. A reward was
offered from Mrs. Bows's goody drawer, but no one found the hat.

Everyone in town tried to find it.

Days went by. Friends and neighbors started bringing Annie purple hats. Ben even offered her one of his hats. "Just so she'll stop crying," he said.

It wasn't long before there were purple hats all over
Annie and Ben's house.
"This one is kind of interesting," said her dad.
Annie began to feel better.

Then one day there was another package at the door.

"Who's it from?" asked Ben.

"I don't know," said Annie.

"Open it," said Ben.

Annie peeked inside and screamed.

It was a purple hat . . .
But this time it was Annie's purple hat.

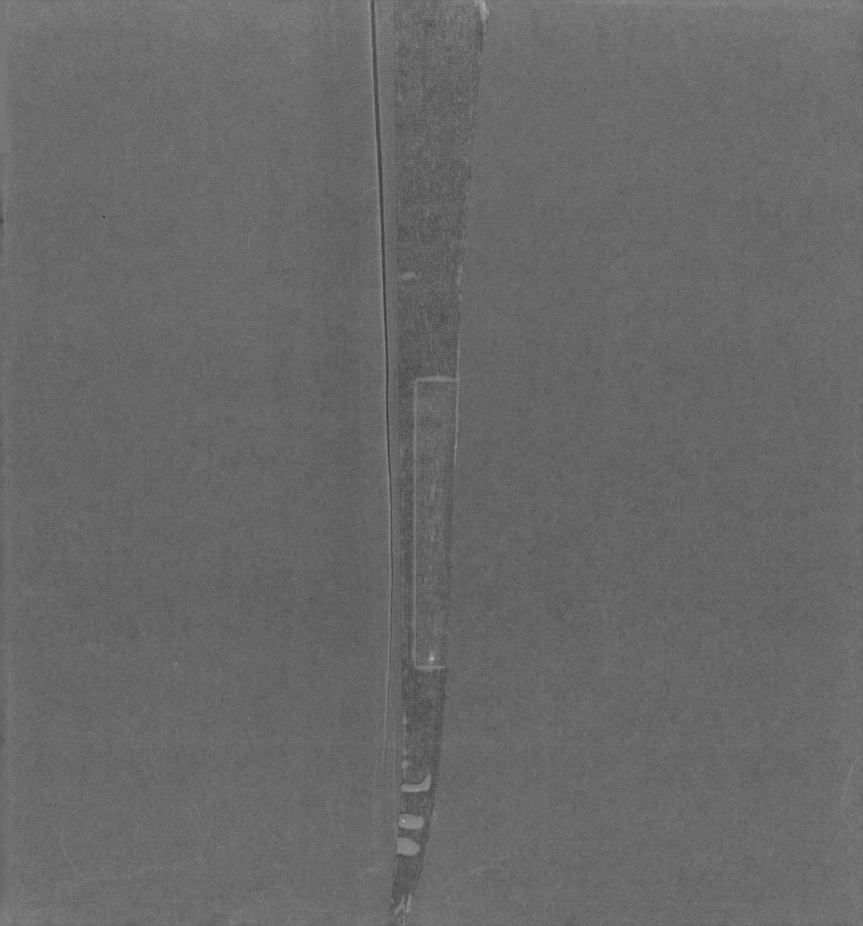